Phoenix Finch is a gender nonconforming, transgender 7-year-old girl who was assigned male at birth (AMAB). She currently identifies with she/her/hers pronouns.

Phoenix knows in her heart who she is, but is struggling with what others will think. She recounts for us, in her own exact words, what it was like for her the first time she went to school wearing a dress.

Phoenix shows us how to be brave and authentic to who we truly are. Her mother shows us to be a safe harbor and provide reassurance so that our children know they are seen and loved unconditionally.

# Phoenix
## goes to school

A Story to Support Transgender and
Gender Diverse Children

Michelle and Phoenix Finch
Illustrated by Sharon Davey

**Jessica Kingsley Publishers**
**London and Philadelphia**

First published in 2018
by Jessica Kingsley Publishers
73 Collier Street
London N1 9BE, UK
and
400 Market Street, Suite 400
Philadelphia, PA 19106, USA

*www.jkp.com*

**Library of Congress Cataloging in Publication Data**
A CIP catalog record for this book is available from the Library of Congress

**British Library Cataloguing in Publication Data**
A CIP catalogue record for this book is available from the British Library

ISBN 978 1 78592 821 5
eISBN 978 1 78450 924 8

Printed and bound in China

*MF & PF: This book is dedicated to all the children and parents out there in the world who are being brave every day, just to be who they are.*

*SD: To Neve and Alex, always.*

I am Phoenix.

This is my family.

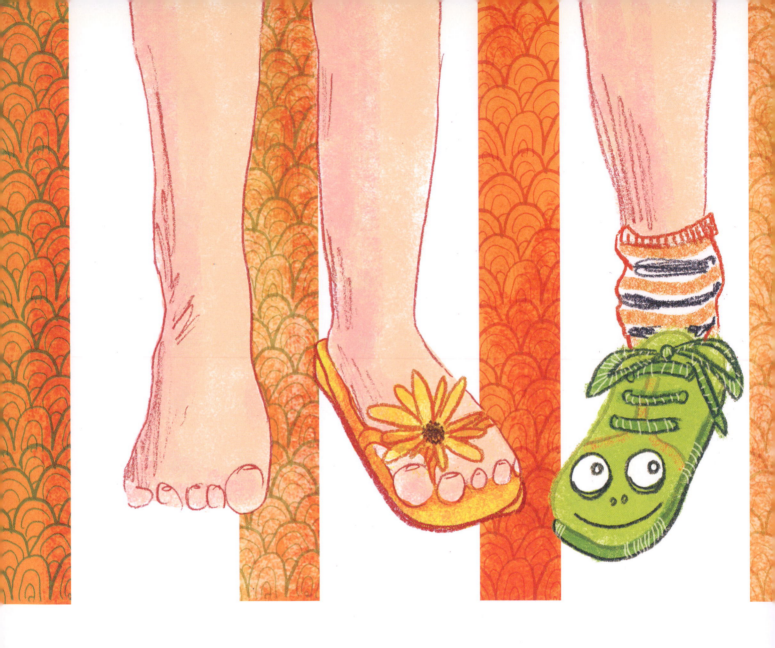

When I was born, the doctor told
my parents they had a baby boy.

But I know I am really a girl. I've always been this way.

Just like I always wake up early.
As soon as my eyes are open,
I pop out of bed and get to work playing.

I build marble runs and play my drums.
I'm racing cars and drawing moons and stars.

I'm twirling, dancing, and doing handstands.
Building towers and drawing flowers…

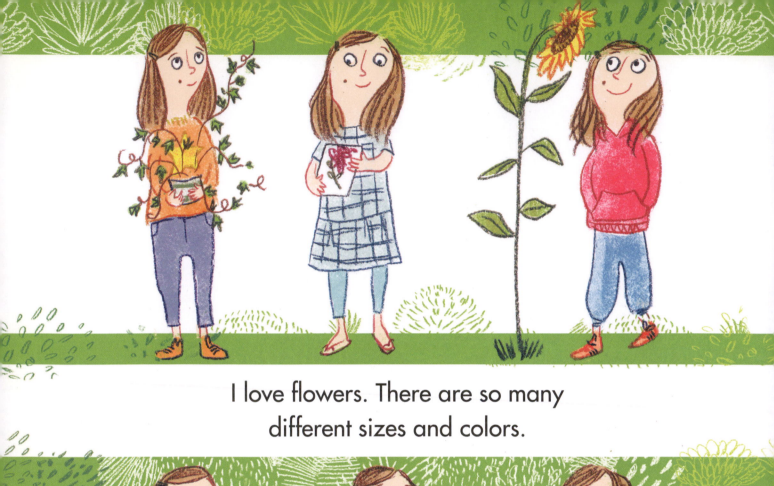

I love flowers. There are so many
different sizes and colors.

Tall and small and each with a special scent!
The purple ones are my favorite.

I love dresses too!
I like the way they swish
and swiggle when I walk.

I like to sparkle and shine in the sun.

Today is my first day of school.
I'm scared to wear my dress to school.

There are bigger kids in the older grades.
They might not understand me.

What if they are bad, bully me, and call me
a baby or a BOY? But, I'm a GIRL!

What if no one will play with me?
Or want to be my friend?

My mommy tells me I'm perfect and to be brave.
"You know who you are," she says.
"Just be yourself and always listen to your heart."

She tells me to remember the pretty flowers that are all different and beautiful in their own way.

I hide behind her legs when we get to school.

My teacher says I look beautiful and
my friend Mia says, "I love your dress."

We spend the afternoon in the school garden.
We plan a royal parade and pick pretty flowers for our crowns.

I make mine of lavender and play a purple princess.

One boy asks, "Are you a boy or are you a girl?"

"GIRL!" I answer. "It's okay to ask."

"Want to watch me do a handstand?" I say.

"Okay," he says. "Wow! What a wonderful handstand, now watch me!"

We ran and played.
The sun warmed my skin, but I felt
cool and happy in my dress.

I felt like me, Phoenix.

I made lots of new friends today.
I felt welcome in my new school.

Tomorrow, I will wear my purple dress.

For additional resources to help parents and
educators talk about gender diversity, visit:
genderspectrum.org or transyouthequality.org

# FOR KIDS

- Out of everyone in the story, who knows Phoenix the best?

- Are the different ways that we express ourselves
  like the different colors of the rainbow?

- Phoenix likes flowers and dresses.
  What are some things that you like?

- Can you think of a time when you knew something
  was true because of how you felt in your heart?

- Were you afraid when you went to your first
  day of school? Why/why not?

- How do you think Phoenix would have felt if the
  kids had laughed at her and teased her?

- Do you think Phoenix had a good first day of school? Why/why not?

- How do you think it made Phoenix feel that her mommy,
  teacher, and friend all were nice to her about her dress?

- Do you think Phoenix is brave? Do you
  remember a time when you were brave?

# FOR GROWN-UPS

Historically, societal norms have presupposed a child's gender based on the external anatomy of the child as a baby. Often, the first question we ask a pregnant mother is, "Are you having a boy or a girl?" but what we now know is that gender is much more complicated than that. The binary system of male/female just doesn't work for many people. In fact, there are a multitude of variations of how humans identify, in relation to gender.

Some children may fall into this category and have a sense from a young age that they don't fit this binary system. Transgender children often have a sense of "other," meaning trans, and may recognize their gender identity does not align to their assigned sex at birth. It is is important to note that not all transgender people are the same and some may identify as transgender after childhood.

Transgender children often express their identity to their family members and caregivers through statements like "My body looks like a boy, but in my heart I feel like a girl." They may demonstrate behavior that was traditionally believed to be the other gender in the binary system—a boy dressing like a girl and vice versa. But we now know that one's identity and gender does not have a prescribed type of clothing or activity associated with it.

Human beings come in all shapes, sizes, colors, and genders! As a species, we are as varied as the colors of the rainbow.

Transgender children, like all children, need the love and support of their family and community to thrive. Providing a safe and supportive environment for transgender children, where they can express who they are in a manner consistent with their gender identity, is essential to helping them to develop positive self-esteem and become happy, healthy members of society.[1]

---

1    Gender Spectrum (2015) *Schools in Transition: A Guide for Supporting Transgender Students in K–12 Schools.* Available at https://www.genderspectrum. org/staging/wp-content/uploads/2015/08/Schools-in-Transition-2015.pdf -page 8, accessed on 20 February 2018.

**Here are some suggested talking points when explaining to children what it means to be transgender:**

- Some people think there is only one way to be a boy or a girl, but there are actually many different ways.

- When we are born, doctors look at our outside body parts and decide to label us as either a boy or a girl. But it is much more complicated than that.

- Sometimes how we look on the outside doesn't match how our brain feels on the inside.

- This doesn't happen a lot, but it does happen. There is nothing wrong with this, it just means this person is unique and beautiful in their own way.

- Some people will change on the outside to match how they feel on the inside. They may change their name, clothes, or other things so that they can be true to who they are.

- The most important thing to remember is that we are all humans, regardless of our gender identity.

- And remember, everyone is born with traits that makes them different from other people. That is what makes people so interesting. We are all different from each other.

- It's okay to ask people how they identify. All we have to do is respect what they tell us about who they are. It is that simple.[2]

---

2   Psychology Today (2016) *How to Talk to Kids About What it Means to be Transgender.* Available at https://www.psychologytoday.com/blog/beyond-pink-and-blue/201605/how-talk-kids-about-what-it-means-be-transgender, accessed on 20 February 2018.

Michelle and Phoenix Finch live in the Bay Area of California, where they enjoy family time at the beach, camping, and pretty much anything outdoors. Phoenix wanted to write a story about her experiences living as a gender nonconforming child, so that other gender nonconforming children "would know they are not alone." Phoenix is 7, loves marble runs, hula hooping, gymnastics, and butterflies. Michelle is a working mom and an active member of the Parents of Transgender Kids community in Marin County. She has trained the parents and faculty at Phoenix's school on gender diversity. This is their first book.

Sharon Davey lives in Surrey, UK with her hilarious family and sassy cat, Eliza Doodle. She illustrates for the children's literature market.